I Can Read!™

BEGINNING 1 READING

THIS *Pinkalicious*

COLLECTION BELONGS TO:

_____

Dear Parent:
Your child's love of reading starts here!

Every child learns to read in a different way and at his or her own speed. Some go back and forth between reading levels and read favorite books again and again. Others read through each level in order. You can help your young reader improve and become more confident by encouraging his or her own interests and abilities. From books your child reads with you to the first books he or she reads alone, there are I Can Read Books for every stage of reading:

SHARED READING
Basic language, word repetition, and whimsical illustrations, ideal for sharing with your emergent reader

BEGINNING READING
Short sentences, familiar words, and simple concepts for children eager to read on their own

READING WITH HELP
Engaging stories, longer sentences, and language play for developing readers

READING ALONE
Complex plots, challenging vocabulary, and high-interest topics for the independent reader

ADVANCED READING
Short paragraphs, chapters, and exciting themes for the perfect bridge to chapter books

I Can Read Books have introduced children to the joy of reading since 1957. Featuring award-winning authors and illustrators and a fabulous cast of beloved characters, I Can Read Books set the standard for beginning readers.

A lifetime of discovery begins with the magical words **"I Can Read!"**

Visit www.icanread.com for information
on enriching your child's reading experience.

This exclusive edition was printed for Kohl's Department Stores, Inc.
(for distribution on behalf of Kohl's Cares, LLC wholly owned) by HarperCollins Publishers.
For information address HarperCollins Children's Books, a division of HarperCollins Publishers,
195 Broadway, New York, NY 10007.
www.icanread.com

ISBN: 978-0-06-285954-9

18 19 20 21 22 SCP 10 9 8 7 6 5 4 3 2 1
First Edition

Kohl's
Style number: 9780062859549
Factory Number 123386
05/2018

I Can Read!

BEGINNING
1
READING

3
TREASURED
STORYBOOKS
for Young Readers!

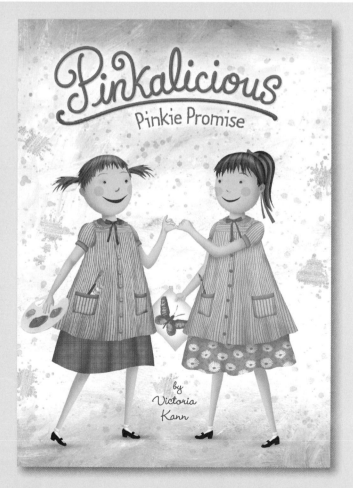

HARPER
An Imprint of HarperCollinsPublishers

TABLE OF CONTENTS

Pinkalicious

School Rules!

To Zelda, Grace, and David
—V.K.

The author gratefully acknowledges
the artistic and editorial contributions
of Daniel Griffo and Susan Hill.

Pinkalicious®
School Rules!

by Victoria Kann

School is okay.
Except for one thing.
When I am at school,
I miss Goldilicious.
Goldie, for short.
Goldie is my unicorn.

I really like my teacher.

His name is Mr. Pushkin.

I have some friends in my class
and I made a new friend yesterday.
But I miss Goldie anyway.

This morning when I woke up
I had a very good idea.
I could bring Goldie to school with me!

School would be
perfectly pinkatastic
with Goldilicious
there, too.

There was a shiny red apple
on Mr. Pushkin's desk.

Goldie took the apple
and nibbled it gently.

Mr. Pushkin heard Goldie munching
and he thought it was me.
"Pinkalicious, there is no eating
until snack time," he said.
"It's the rule."

"It's not me," I said.
"It's Goldilicious, my unicorn!
She didn't eat much for breakfast,"
I added.

Mr. Pushkin smiled.

He took me aside

and he told me that unicorns

are not allowed in school.

"It's the rule," he said.

Rules are something

I do not love about school.

And I really do not love

the rule about no unicorns.

I began to cry a little.

I cried a little harder.
"Okay, Pinkalicious,"
said Mr. Pushkin.
"Your unicorn may stay,
just this once."

I stopped crying.

In fact, I clapped and twirled.

"But if your unicorn stays, you must teach her the rules," Mr. Pushkin said. "Do you think you can do that?"

"Yes!" I said.
"I know I can!"

At reading time,
Goldilicious was very quiet.

Goldilicious helped me with my math.
Unicorns are very good at counting.

When it was time for recess,
I showed Goldilicious
how to line up by the door.
Goldilicious did not push
or wiggle or cut the line at all.

Goldilicious played nicely
with the other kids.

Everyone had so much fun
with Goldie and me.

I didn't know I had
so many friends at school!

Soon it was time to go home.
Goldie got my backpack
off its hook.

"Tell me, Pinkalicious,"
said Mr. Pushkin.
"Did you and your unicorn
have a good day?"
"We sure did!" I said.

"School rules!"

Pinkalicious®

Fashion Fun

To Ellen
—V.K.

The author gratefully acknowledges
the artistic and editorial contributions of
Daniel Griffo and Kamilla Benko.

Pinkalicious®
Fashion Fun

by Victoria Kann

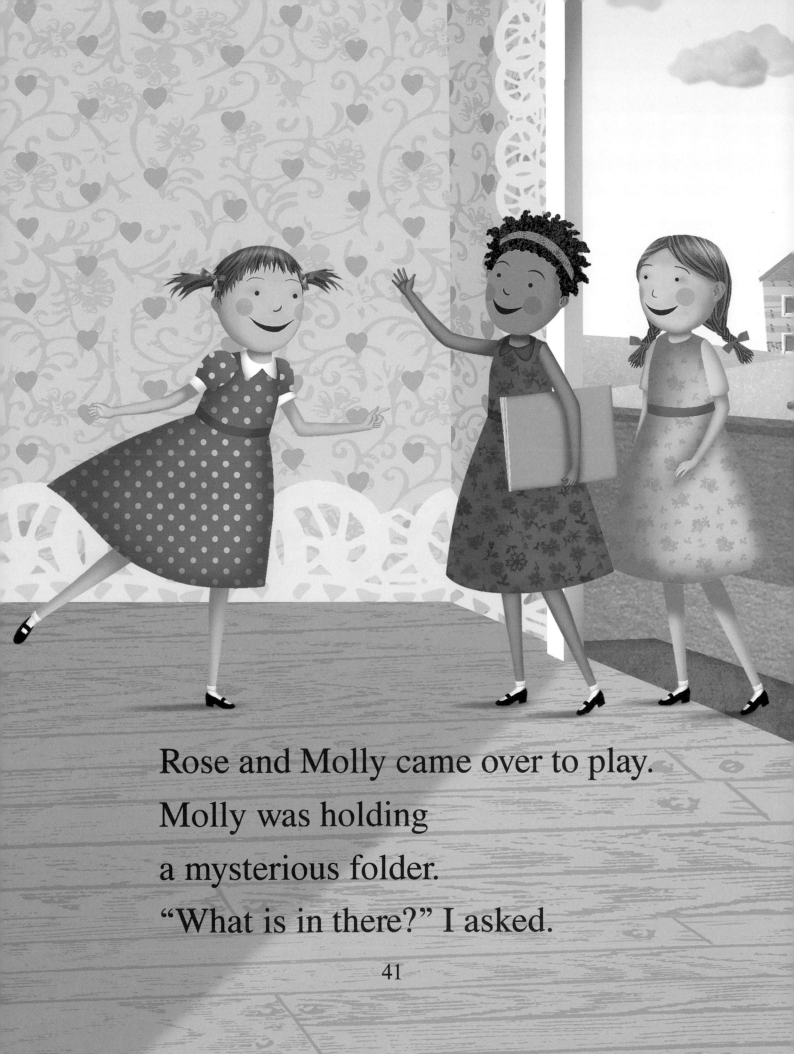

Rose and Molly came over to play.
Molly was holding
a mysterious folder.
"What is in there?" I asked.

"They're pictures
of designer clothing
and fashion shows that I've collected
from magazines," Molly explained.

"Those are beautiful outfits!" Rose said.

"I want dresses like that," I said.

"Mommy has a dress
like the one in that picture.
Let's look in her closet," I said.
"We can have our own
fashion show!"

Just then, Mommy came in.

"What are you doing?" Mommy asked.

"My clothes are not for playtime!"

"We're fashion designers," I said.
"Please use your imaginations,
not my clothing," said Mommy.

"Ew, imaginary clothes!"
said Rose.
"Please play in your room,
not my closet!" said Mommy.

We looked at the pictures again.
"I like those shoes
with bows," I said.

"The bows look like pasta,"
said Molly.
"I have an idea!" I said.

"We need glue!" I said.

"Let's get twist ties!" said Rose.

"Don't forget glitter!" said Molly.

"What are you doing?" asked Peter.
"Can I do it, too?"
I thought about it.

"You can be a photographer," I said.

"Yes!" he yelled.

"Say cupcake and smile!"

The doorbell rang.
My friends' mothers
were here to pick them up.
"Have a seat," said Mommy.
"The girls have a surprise for you."

"Are you ready?" I asked my friends.
"It's showtime!"

"Welcome to our fashion show!"
Rose said as we paraded
into the living room.

56

"We used things
around the house
to make our clothes,"
I added.

"Look at my newspaper
and coffee-filter pants!"
said Molly.

"The flowers on my vest
are cupcake liners," said Rose.

"My dress is made
from Bubble Wrap!" I said.
Click! went Peter's camera.

"Bravo!" Rose's mommy cheered.
"Show off your outfits and twirl!"
We twirled faster and faster!

Paper, ribbons,
and cupcake liners went flying!
Peter got closer and closer,
trying to get the perfect picture. . . .

61

POP, POP, POP, POP!

My dress was ruined!
I almost started to cry,
but then I heard clapping!

"Marvelous!" Molly's mommy said.
"You made a dress
that can be worn two different ways,
and now we can see your
sparkly macaroni shoes!

"If you stick with it," she said,
"you'll have a career in fashion!
I love how you used food
in your designs."
"Oh yes!" I said. I was inspired.

I smiled and grabbed my sketchbook.

I had an idea:

a cupcake dress!

I wonder if I could use real frosting.

Pinkalicious®

Pinkie Promise

For Marjorie and Bob,
thank you for your support and guidance.
—V.K.

The author gratefully acknowledges
the artistic and editorial contributions
of Daniel Griffo and Susan Hill.

Pinkalicious®

Pinkie Promise

by Victoria Kann

I was making a picture
for my teacher, Mr. Pushkin.
I ran out of my favorite color.

I asked my friend Alison
if I could borrow her paints.
"Just don't use up all the pink," she said.
"I won't," I said.
"I promise."

I worked very hard on the picture.
It looked good.

I gave the picture to Mr. Pushkin.

"What a terrific painting!" he said.

"It's so pink."

"You mean it's pinkerrific!" I said.

Alison was coming over
to get her paint set.

Some of the colors were empty.

Uh-oh.

What was I going to do?

"Um . . . I'm sorry, Alison," I said.

"By mistake I used up all the pink."

Alison frowned.

"You also used up all the red

and the white," she said.

"Well, red and white make pink,

so really it's all pink," I said.

Alison was angry.

"You said you wouldn't use up
all the pink paint!" said Alison.
"You promised."
"I'm really really sorry, Alison,"
I said again.
Alison took her paint set
and walked away.

Alison did not sit with me at lunch.
I sat alone.

I ate my jelly sandwich.
Jelly does not taste pink-a-yummy
if you are eating all by yourself.

Then I thought of something.
I went back to the classroom.
I made Alison a card to apologize.

"This card is very blue,"
I said to Alison.
"There were no other colors.
Almost everybody is out of pink."

"Thanks for the card," Alison said.
"It's not just beautiful, it's bluetiful."

"Alison," I asked,
"can we still be friends?"

"Of course we're friends,
Pinkalicious," Alison said.
"I'm sorry I got angry
about the paint.
I won't get so mad next time."

I was so happy!

"Let's play this weekend!" I said.

When Alison came over to play,
I had a surprise for her.

I gave Alison a new tube of paint.
"It's not even my birthday!"
said Alison.
"And that's not all," I said.
"Guess what?"

We got ice cream!

We shared a pink peppermint ice cream sundae with raspberry swirl syrup.

The sundae had two cherries on top
so we could each have our own.
Some things are just too hard to share!

PLEASING POMEGRANATE PUNCH

MAGENTA MINT MANGO

PINK PEPPERMINT

PLUM PINK PERFECTION

"Let's always be friends,"
Alison said.
"Yes, that would be funtastic,"
I said.

"Let's make it a pinkie promise!"
we said at the same time.
"Pinkie promise last forever,"
I said happily.